Christmas at Silver Creek Ranch: A Second Chance Cowboy Romance

A Heartwarming Holiday Romance in the Country – Book 1 in the Christmas Western Love Stories

James Holloway

Contents

Foreword	v
Chapter 1	1
Chapter 2	6
Chapter 3	12
Chapter 4	18
Chapter 5	22
Chapter 6	28
Chapter 7	34
Chapter 8	40
Chapter 9	44
Chapter 10	48
Chapter 11	52
Also by James Holloway	57

Foreword

Snow fell gently over Silver Creek, covering the ranch fields in a soft blanket of white that seemed to glow under the pale December sun. Abby stood on the front porch of the Harper ranch, wrapped in a cozy sweater, her breath visible in the frosty air as she watched the flakes drift down. The familiar landscape was a comforting sight, though one she hadn't expected to love so deeply. A year ago, she'd stood on this same porch, feeling like a stranger in her own home. Now, as the quiet holiday morning settled around her, she felt more grounded, more certain than ever.

Inside, the house buzzed with activity and warmth. Friends, neighbors, and family gathered around the old fireplace, laughing and sharing memories, their voices blending with the faint sound of Christmas carols playing on the radio. Abby's father, Bill, sat in his armchair, chatting with the ranch hands, a relaxed, contented smile on his face.

Abby smiled, thinking of everything it had taken to get here. She'd spent years in New York, chasing a life that had once felt like her calling. She'd convinced herself that the excitement of the city, the thrill of her career, and the glow of skyscrapers were what she wanted most. Silver Creek, she thought back then, was just a place she'd come from—not the place she was going.

But that Christmas Eve a year ago had changed everything. She'd returned to help her father and ended up finding more than she'd ever imagined: her family, her community, and the love she'd been searching for in all the wrong places. Luke had waited for her, steady as the mountains that surrounded them, and his patience, his love, had been the anchor that finally brought her home.

Now, as Luke joined her on the porch, slipping his hand into hers, Abby glanced up at him with a smile, her heart filled with gratitude and the quiet certainty that she was exactly where she was meant to be.

> *This story is about finding your way back to the people and places that shape you, even when life pulls you in different directions. It's a journey that took me from the neon lights of New York City back to the quiet, open skies of Silver Creek—a journey that led me to rediscover the meaning of home, family, and love. I hope that through Abby's story, you'll find a reminder of the places, people, and dreams that truly matter.*

So, grab a warm cup of cocoa, settle in, and join me in Silver Creek, where Christmas spirit, love, and community have a way of bringing us all home.

1

The Return

Abby Harper swiped a hand through her hair and sighed as the screen before her glowed with endless rows of spreadsheets. The holidays were supposed to be festive, but in her office overlooking the steel-grey cityscape, they felt more like just another job. Twinkling lights on nearby buildings and wreaths on doors only seemed to remind her how hollow she felt. She had always loved Christmas, but ever since moving to New York, she felt herself slipping further and further away from that warmth. This year, with her breakup fresh in her mind, she felt it more than ever.

"Another deadline," she muttered to herself, eyes drifting to a photo on her desk—a rare family picture of her younger self grinning atop a horse, her dad standing proudly by her side. In that moment, Silver Creek and its wide, open spaces felt like a memory too far removed from her world of skyscrapers and subway trains.

The phone broke her reverie, buzzing insistently. Abby ignored it at first, assuming it was yet another work call. But the caller was persistent. Finally, she glanced at the screen, her brows furrowing as she saw her father's number flashing across the display.

"Hello?" she answered, a hint of surprise coloring her voice.

"Abby, sweetheart," came the familiar, gravelly voice. But something in her father's tone made her stomach twist. Bill Harper sounded tired, more so than usual.

"Dad? Is everything okay?" she asked, worry creeping into her tone.

There was a pause on the other end, and in that silence, Abby could almost picture her father leaning back in his worn leather armchair, hesitating. Bill Harper was never one to ask for help; he was as steady as the mountains surrounding Silver Creek.

"Well," he began slowly, as if choosing his words carefully, "I didn't want to worry you. But... I've been feeling a bit under the weather."

"Under the weather?" Abby echoed, her heart pounding. "Since when?"

"Couple of weeks now. Doctor says I need to take it easy. Not exactly easy when the ranch needs looking after," he admitted, a trace of stubbornness edging into his voice. "But, uh... I'd be lying if I said I didn't need some help around here."

There it was, the invitation she hadn't expected. Abby felt a flood of emotions rush over her—guilt, worry, and that pang of homesickness she'd tried so hard to ignore for years.

"I... I'll be there soon, Dad," she said, the words spilling out before she had a chance to second-guess them.

And just like that, she found herself booking a last-minute flight to Wyoming, stepping away from her skyscrapers and presentations. The decision felt both impulsive and oddly relieving, though a hint of dread bubbled up beneath her relief.

Returning to Silver Creek wasn't just about her father. It was about confronting the life she'd left behind and the fractured pieces she still carried with her.

THE TRIP back to Silver Creek was a blur of connections and layovers, but as the small plane touched down and the chilly mountain air hit her face, Abby felt a jolt of something she couldn't quite name. The town looked much the same as she remembered it—snow-capped and quiet, a place that seemed to resist the rush of time. But Abby could feel the distance she'd created over the years. She wasn't the same girl who'd once dreamed of taking over her father's ranch.

As she drove the old truck she'd rented from town, winding her way through the snow-dusted hills, her thoughts drifted. Every turn in the road brought back memories—riding horses in the open pastures, helping her dad mend fences, her mother baking pies in the farmhouse kitchen. Abby swallowed hard, trying to push those memories back into the past where they belonged.

The Harper Ranch loomed ahead, its white fences gleaming against the snow, though there was a worn-out, weather-beaten look to it now. She noticed patches of the fencing in need of repair and fewer cattle than she remembered. A pang of worry cut through her as she turned into the driveway, the familiar crunch of gravel under the tires stirring a bittersweet familiarity.

Abby parked the truck and stepped out, taking a deep breath. The cold air filled her lungs, carrying the scent of pine and old leather, smells that reminded her of simpler times. She closed her eyes, her heart thudding with anticipation, nerves, and a sliver of dread.

"Abby?" a weak voice called, and she turned to see her father standing in the doorway of the old farmhouse, looking smaller and older than she remembered. His hair was grayer, his frame thinner, but his face lit up with that same, warm smile she'd missed so much.

"Dad!" Abby ran up the steps and wrapped him in a hug, careful to hold back her worry.

"Well, don't squeeze the life out of me just yet," Bill chuckled, pulling back to look at her. "You're a sight for sore eyes."

The warmth in his eyes was comforting, but she could see the weariness beneath it. His hands shook slightly as he led her into the house, and Abby noticed how the place seemed quieter, emptier. Her heart ached as she realized just how much her father had been through alone.

"So, what's the doctor saying?" Abby asked gently once they'd settled into the living room, a fire crackling in the hearth.

"Oh, just a bit of a scare. I'm fine now, though," he shrugged, waving it off. But Abby wasn't fooled; the way he winced when he moved spoke volumes.

As she looked around, her gaze settled on a few papers scattered on the table—bills, letters from the bank. Abby's eyes flickered back to her father, her worry deepening.

"Dad, why didn't you tell me things had gotten this tough?"

He sighed, looking away for a moment before meeting her gaze. "Didn't want to worry you, Abby. I know you've got your life in the city, and it's not your responsibility to take on the ranch. But... I can't lie, it's been hard keeping up."

Just as she was about to reassure him, the sound of footsteps on the porch broke the silence. She turned to see a tall, rugged figure standing in the doorway, and her heart skipped a beat.

Luke Grayson.

The last person she'd expected to see. With his worn Stetson in one hand and a faintly guarded expression, Luke stepped inside. "Bill," he greeted, nodding to her father, then his gaze shifted to Abby. His eyes widened slightly, but he covered it with a nod. "Abby."

"Luke," she replied, her voice steady, though her heart raced. They hadn't seen each other since she'd left Silver Creek, and she hadn't thought much about him until now. But standing before him, she felt the unresolved tension simmering between them.

"Just wanted to check in on you, Bill. Make sure you were all set," Luke said, casting a lingering look at Abby before turning back to her father.

"Appreciate it, Luke," Bill said, a warm smile breaking the tension. "You know, Abby's here to help out now. Might be a little easier on me."

Luke's eyes returned to Abby, something unreadable in his gaze. "Well, it's good you're back," he said, a hint of warmth softening his tone. "The ranch could use it."

Abby felt a swell of conflicting emotions—pride, discomfort, and something else she wasn't ready to name. The Silver Creek she'd left behind was no longer just a memory; it was a reality, full of challenges, unspoken words, and one unresolved past standing right before her.

As Luke tipped his hat and turned to leave, Abby felt the weight of everything she'd come back to—the ranch, her father's health, and the unmistakable pull of a life she thought she'd left behind for good.

2

Home Again

Abby stepped out of the truck, her boots crunching on the gravel as she took in the view before her. The Harper Ranch, blanketed in a soft layer of snow, looked almost dreamlike in the late afternoon light. The sight tugged at something deep within her, a nostalgia she hadn't anticipated. The familiar curve of the driveway, the barn looming proudly to the left, and the cozy little farmhouse nestled in the center—each detail felt like a piece of herself she'd left behind years ago.

She closed her eyes for a moment, letting the crisp winter air fill her lungs. It smelled of pine and old leather, with a faint hint of the woodsmoke that drifted from the farmhouse chimney. Memories flashed before her mind like a flickering film reel—days spent riding her horse across the open pasture, laughing with her mother in the kitchen as they baked pies, and nights spent watching the stars with her father, his stories of the land weaving a deep sense of belonging in her young heart.

As she took a few steps toward the porch, Abby noticed the small details that spoke to the ranch's struggles. The fence along the corral was worn, a few boards missing, and the once vibrant red paint on the barn was faded and chipped. A familiar ache settled in her chest as she realized how much her father had been dealing with alone. She shook her head, steeling herself. There would be time to worry about the ranch's state later; right now, she just needed to see him.

"Dad?" she called, her voice carrying through the stillness. She pushed open the front door and was instantly wrapped in the scent of cedarwood and faint traces of her father's aftershave. The house was dimly lit, with the low glow of a fire flickering in the hearth.

"Abby?" came a voice from the kitchen, slightly hoarse but unmistakably her father's. She felt a surge of warmth at the sound. Stepping into the small but familiar living room, she found her father standing by the kitchen table, leaning slightly on his cane. He looked thinner than she remembered, his frame a little hunched, but his face lit up with a bright smile that erased years from his features.

"You're really here," he said, his voice soft with disbelief.

"Of course I am, Dad." Abby crossed the room in a few quick steps and wrapped her arms around him, swallowing the lump that had risen in her throat. She could feel how frail he'd become, the strength that had once defined him now softened by age and illness. Pulling back slightly, she searched his face, her heart clenching at the new lines etched around his eyes and mouth.

He gave her a sheepish smile. "Didn't mean to worry you, sweetheart. But I suppose a bit of help wouldn't hurt. This place has its demands, you know."

She forced a smile, wanting to reassure him despite the worry gnawing at her. "Well, you've got it now," she said, squeezing his hand. "You're stuck with me."

They settled down in the living room, and as Abby looked around, memories flooded back, each corner of the room filled with echoes of her past. The mantle was still lined with the same family photos, including one of her and her mother on her first pony ride, her mother's hand steady on her back. Abby felt the familiar pang of loss as her gaze lingered on the image. Her mother had been gone for so long now, but her presence still lingered in the little details scattered throughout the house—the handmade quilt on the back of the couch, the antique clock on the mantle, the jar of dried lavender her mother had always kept in the kitchen.

"So," she said, trying to lighten the mood, "what kind of trouble has this place been up to while I was gone?"

Bill chuckled, though there was a heaviness in his gaze. "Oh, you know, the usual. Cattle prices down, fence repairs adding up, that kind of thing. Been a tough few years." He gave a small shrug, the weight of it all evident even in that simple gesture.

Abby felt a pang of guilt. She'd been so absorbed in her own life, so consumed with her job and her personal dramas, that she'd barely checked in on him beyond the occasional phone call. Her gaze drifted over to the table, where a stack of bills peeked out from under an old Western novel.

"Dad, why didn't you tell me it had gotten this tough?" she asked, her voice barely above a whisper.

Bill shook his head, offering her a weary smile. "Didn't want to worry you, sweetheart. Besides, I knew you were busy building your life out there. Didn't see the point in dragging you back to an old ranch when you've got dreams to chase."

Abby looked down, guilt prickling her. The ranch might have been old, but it was more than just land. It was her father's legacy, her childhood home, and, in so many ways, a part of her that she'd tried to push aside.

Before she could find the words to respond, there was a knock on the door, followed by the sound of boots on the porch. Abby looked up, her heart giving an unexpected jolt as she recognized the tall, broad figure stepping into the entryway.

"Bill, thought I'd stop by and make sure you were all set for the night," came the deep, familiar voice of Luke Grayson.

Abby's breath caught as Luke entered, his gaze briefly locking onto hers before he shifted his focus to her father. He was still the same rugged cowboy she remembered, his presence filling the room in a way that was both comforting and unsettling. She hadn't seen him since the day she'd left for the city, and the years had only seemed to add a quiet strength to his demeanor, the same intense look in his eyes softened slightly by the wisdom of age.

"Luke," she said, her voice steady despite the fluttering in her chest. The air between them felt thick with unspoken words, and she wasn't sure if it was her memories or something more that made her heart race.

"Abby," he replied, nodding in her direction, his tone polite yet guarded. She could see a flicker of something in his eyes—surprise, perhaps, or maybe something deeper, buried beneath the surface.

"Good to have you back," he added, his voice carrying a faint warmth that surprised her.

"Thanks," she murmured, managing a small smile. They stood there in awkward silence, each aware of the weight of their shared history, neither willing to breach it just yet.

"Luke's been a big help around here," Bill said, breaking the silence. "Since my health went south, he's been looking out for me and the ranch."

Abby turned to Luke, a mixture of gratitude and discomfort bubbling up. "Thank you, Luke. I appreciate you helping my dad."

Luke nodded, his gaze steady. "It's no trouble. Bill's always been like family to me. Just doing what I can."

He looked around, his eyes landing on the same signs of disrepair that had caught her attention earlier. "The ranch could use a bit of TLC," he added, his voice thoughtful.

She felt a surge of defensiveness, an instinctive need to protect her father's pride and legacy. "We'll get it back in shape," she replied, a touch more firmly than she'd intended. "I'm here now, so I can help."

Luke's eyebrows lifted slightly, a hint of a smirk playing on his lips. "Glad to hear it," he said, his tone carrying an edge she couldn't quite decipher.

Bill, sensing the tension, gave a chuckle. "Well, I think the two of you together will whip this place back into shape in no time."

Luke shifted, glancing back toward the door. "I should get going. Let you two catch up. But, Bill, if you need anything, just give me a shout."

"Will do, son," Bill said, nodding gratefully. "Thank you, Luke."

Luke gave Abby one last look before tipping his hat. "Take care, Abby."

"Yeah," she replied softly. "You too."

As the door clicked shut behind him, Abby let out a breath she hadn't realized she'd been holding. Her father's eyes twinkled with a knowing smile as he leaned back in his chair, watching her with quiet amusement.

"So," he said, crossing his arms. "Looks like you two still have some sparks flying between you."

Abby's cheeks flushed. "Dad, don't start," she protested, though she could tell from his smile that he wasn't going to let it go so easily.

"Just saying, sweetheart. Man like Luke—a good man—doesn't come around every day." He sighed, glancing around the room, a faraway look in his eyes. "Sometimes, we don't realize what we have until it's gone."

She let out a small sigh, feeling the weight of his words. Her father had always loved this ranch, poured every ounce of his soul into it. But time had taken its toll, and seeing Luke step in when she wasn't there only added to her guilt. She'd spent so long chasing a life outside of Silver Creek, desperate to build something of her own, but she hadn't realized how much she'd lost in the process.

"I'll help with the ranch, Dad," she said, a renewed determination filling her. "We'll get it back to what it used to be."

Bill's face softened, and he reached out, squeezing her hand. "That's all I needed to hear."

But as Abby settled in that night, lying awake in her old bedroom with the sounds of the ranch around her, she couldn't shake the memory of Luke's gaze or the undeniable spark between them. Silver Creek was filled with memories she'd tried to bury, but it seemed they were determined to resurface, pulling her back to the life—and the people—she'd left behind.

3

Old Feelings, New Challenges

The next morning, Abby woke up to the soft, golden light streaming through the old lace curtains in her childhood room. She took a moment, lying there and listening to the familiar sounds of the ranch waking up—the faint lowing of cattle, the clatter of horses' hooves, and the distant hum of machinery. It was peaceful, nostalgic even, but the peacefulness only made her feel more like a stranger in her own home.

With a sigh, she pulled herself out of bed, glancing around the room she hadn't set foot in for years. Her old posters, curling at the edges, still hung on the walls, and the bookshelf was lined with the novels she used to devour on rainy afternoons. Abby ran her fingers over the worn spines, her mind slipping back to a different time—a time when her world revolved around school, chores, and sneaking out with Luke to escape her father's curfew.

A familiar warmth—and a twinge of sadness—filled her chest

at the thought of him. They'd been inseparable back then, sharing everything from dreams of leaving Silver Creek to whispers of a future that, at one time, they'd imagined would always include each other. But those were teenage dreams, she reminded herself, before life and ambition had swept her away, leaving Luke and the ranch as a distant memory. Yet, seeing him now, Abby realized that leaving hadn't made the memories fade as much as she'd thought.

With a sigh, she tore herself away from the memories and headed downstairs, finding her father already in the kitchen, stirring a pot of oatmeal.

"Morning, Dad," she greeted, pressing a quick kiss to his cheek.

"Morning, sweetheart," he replied, glancing over his shoulder with a smile. "Good to see you're finally up. Thought you'd sleep the day away."

Abby rolled her eyes, but there was a smile tugging at her lips. "I'm here, aren't I? Besides, you're supposed to be the one taking it easy."

Her father chuckled, a mischievous gleam in his eyes. "Can't keep an old rancher down for long. Besides, I figured you'd want to get a look at things yourself, see what we're up against."

As they ate breakfast, her father filled her in on the ranch's struggles. The low prices for cattle, the rising costs of feed, and the way a few harsh winters had taken their toll. Abby listened, nodding, and taking mental notes, though part of her was still unsure if she was ready to jump back into ranch life. She'd built a different life in the city—one where she knew the rules, knew what to expect. Here, on the ranch, everything felt unfamiliar yet uncomfortably close.

"So, what's the plan, then?" she asked finally, trying to keep her tone light. "I'm guessing you've got a few ideas up your sleeve?"

Bill gave her a sly smile, pausing for a moment before answering. "Well, funny you should ask. Actually, there's something I'd like you to help with. It's something I think you'd be perfect for."

"Oh?" Abby arched an eyebrow, feeling both intrigued and wary.

Her father leaned forward, his eyes glinting with a spark she hadn't seen in a while. "The Silver Creek Christmas Rodeo. It's only a few weeks away, and Luke's been taking the lead on organizing it, but I thought you could step in and help him. It would be good for you... and for the town. It's one of Silver Creek's biggest traditions, and I'd love to see you get involved."

Abby hesitated, torn between the urge to say no and the realization that this meant a lot to her father. She'd loved the rodeo as a kid, looking forward to it every year, and helping with it could be a way to give back to the town. But working with Luke? The thought sent a ripple of both excitement and apprehension through her. Could she really work alongside him, with all those old feelings lurking beneath the surface?

"Well," she said slowly, glancing down at her hands. "If it means that much to you, Dad... I guess I could help out. Just don't expect any miracles."

Her father chuckled, looking genuinely relieved. "That's all I'm asking for, sweetheart. Just you being here means the world to me."

LUKE

That same morning, Luke was at the corral, checking on the young horses they'd lined up for the rodeo. He brushed one of the horses absently, his thoughts drifting back to Abby's arrival the day before. He hadn't expected to see her walk through that door, and the sight of her had thrown him more than he'd wanted to admit. The years had only sharpened her beauty, her confidence, but he sensed something guarded behind her smile.

Christmas at Silver Creek Ranch: A Second Chance Cowboy Romance

He hadn't realized, until seeing her, just how much of his past was tangled up in her. The girl he'd once loved, the woman he'd watched leave without so much as a look back. He'd tried to move on, focused on the ranch, on helping Bill, and on building something real here in Silver Creek. But there had always been that nagging thought in the back of his mind, a whisper of what could have been.

The memory of her laugh, her easy smile, and the way she'd looked at him with that spark in her eyes—all of it still lingered, despite his best efforts to let it go. And now, just when he thought he'd buried those old feelings, here she was, standing in front of him like a ghost from a life he'd almost forgotten.

Luke sighed, patting the horse's neck as he tried to push the thoughts away. He'd always known she was meant for bigger things, that the city had called to her in a way Silver Creek never could. But seeing her here now, he couldn't help but feel a small, foolish hope that maybe—just maybe—she'd decide to stay. Though deep down, he knew it was a dangerous hope to hold.

Bill's familiar voice broke his thoughts, and he turned to see the older man making his way toward him, looking slightly more energetic than usual.

"Morning, Luke," Bill called, a warm smile on his face.

"Morning, Bill," Luke replied, tipping his hat. "You're looking spry today. Abby must be rubbing off on you."

Bill chuckled, shaking his head. "It's good having her back. I'd forgotten what it's like to have the house filled with her chatter." He paused, a thoughtful look crossing his face. "Actually, I was hoping you'd be alright with her helping out at the rodeo."

Luke's heart skipped a beat, but he kept his expression neutral. "Of course, she's welcome to help. I could use an extra set of hands, especially with all the details we need to iron out."

Bill nodded, a sly smile tugging at the corners of his mouth.

"Figured you wouldn't mind too much. You two always did work well together, even when you were young."

Luke managed a small smile, though a part of him wished he could shake off the sense of inevitability that Abby's presence seemed to bring. "We'll see how it goes."

Abby

By the afternoon, Abby found herself standing in the rodeo arena, feeling a mixture of nostalgia and unease. The place hadn't changed a bit—the grandstand with its faded paint, the dusty arena, and the row of wooden stalls lining the far end, each one familiar as an old friend. She remembered sneaking out here with Luke, laughing as they plotted ways to impress the crowd with their roping and riding skills.

A voice behind her pulled her from her thoughts, and she turned to see Luke approaching, his steady gaze catching her off guard.

"Glad you could make it," he said, his tone polite but distant. "Figured we should get a head start on the setup if we're going to have everything ready by Christmas."

"Right," Abby replied, swallowing the awkwardness that seemed to hang between them. "Where do you want me?"

Luke pointed to a stack of banners and supplies by the stands. "We'll start with the decorations, then go over the event schedule. I figured you could help with some of the details—the things I'm not as good at."

Abby nodded, though she could feel the tension between them thickening as they moved into the work. They spoke only when necessary, a few polite exchanges about decorations and setup, but mostly, they worked in silence. Yet, despite the distance, Abby found herself noticing the familiar ease in Luke's movements, the way he instinctively took the lead but checked in with her as if inviting her into the rhythm of his work. It was different from the city's rush; here, everything felt grounded, real.

At one point, as they hung a banner along the fence, Luke looked over, catching her gaze. "I'm surprised you agreed to help," he admitted quietly, his eyes searching hers. "Didn't think you'd want to get involved with something like this."

Abby hesitated, her heart pounding. "Honestly, I wasn't sure I wanted to," she said, her voice soft. "But it means a lot to my dad... and I guess a part of me missed it, too. Missed being part of something real."

He nodded, a hint of a smile touching his lips. "Glad to hear it. Silver Creek's always had a way of bringing people back."

4

The Silver Creek Spirit

Abby found herself spending more and more time at the rodeo grounds, knee-deep in decorations and logistics with Luke. Though she'd initially agreed to help for her father's sake, she was beginning to feel a tug of something she hadn't felt in a long time—a sense of belonging. Even if she and Luke seemed to clash on almost every decision.

"Abby, the barrels should be lined up along the north fence. They're tradition!" Luke said, his arms crossed, exasperation in his eyes.

Abby planted her hands on her hips, not backing down. "They'll look better near the entrance, Luke. It's more inviting."

He let out a sigh, shaking his head. "You and your city ideas..."

"Oh, like everything here has to stay exactly the same?" Abby shot back, half-smiling, half-frustrated.

For a moment, they locked eyes, and Abby noticed a flicker of amusement behind his irritation. She caught herself smiling, realizing that their banter had become an oddly familiar rhythm, a push and pull that somehow brought them closer rather than pushing them apart.

They spent the next few days in a whirlwind of rodeo preparations, stringing up twinkling lights along the fence, setting up hay bales for seating, and painting signs for the different events. Though they argued over every detail, Abby couldn't deny that they worked well together. Luke's steady, practical approach balanced out her eye for detail and charm, and slowly, they found a rhythm that worked.

One evening, as they were packing up the last of the supplies, Luke nodded toward the Christmas lights they'd hung around the arena. "Looks good. Gotta admit, your ideas brought the place to life."

Abby glanced at him, surprised by the compliment. "Thanks," she said softly, her heart warming at the gesture.

They stood in comfortable silence, watching the lights twinkle against the darkening sky. For a moment, it felt like they were back in high school, just two kids dreaming under the stars. The years seemed to fade away, and Abby felt that familiar pull, the one she'd tried so hard to ignore.

As the days passed, Abby found herself drawn deeper into Silver Creek's holiday spirit. She helped set up booths at the town's Christmas market, laughing with familiar faces as they reminisced about the good old days. She even took on the job of organizing a gingerbread bake-off for the kids, enlisting her father to judge—a task he took on with far too much gusto, making Abby laugh as he sampled each cookie with exaggerated seriousness.

When she wasn't at the market or the rodeo grounds, she found herself decorating the Harper ranch. She and her father brought down the old boxes of Christmas decorations, dusting off each ornament and wreath as memories poured back. They strung lights around the barn and along the porch railing, their laughter and conversation filling the crisp, cold air.

"You know," her father said one evening, as they put up the last string of lights, "it's been a long time since I've seen you this happy."

Abby glanced at him, caught off guard. "I am happy," she said, surprised by the realization as much as her father was.

Bill chuckled softly, resting a hand on her shoulder. "Silver Creek has always had a way of getting into your bones. Makes you wonder if you ever really left."

Abby looked away, her mind turning back to Luke and the ease they'd found in each other's company, despite their disagreements. Maybe her father was right. Maybe there was a part of her that had never truly left this place.

OVER THE NEXT WEEK, she and Luke continued working side by side on the rodeo preparations, their moments of disagreement gradually giving way to a comfortable camaraderie. One evening, after a long day of setting up, they sat on the bleachers, sharing a thermos of hot chocolate under the stars.

"So," Luke began, after a moment's silence, "are you really just here until your dad's feeling better?"

Abby hesitated, feeling the weight of his question. "I... I'm not sure, to be honest." She looked down at the cup in her hands. "The city has been my whole life for so long. But being here, with my dad... and even working with you on this rodeo..." She trailed off, a soft smile on her face. "I'm not ready to decide just yet."

Luke nodded, his gaze thoughtful. "Silver Creek has a way of doing that. Makes you see what really matters."

She glanced over at him, meeting his steady gaze. The connection between them felt as real and undeniable as the stars above, rekindling memories she'd tried to bury. She could feel the warmth in his eyes, the quiet patience he had always held, waiting for her, even now. But before she could say anything, the distant chime of a bell from the church down the road reminded them of the late hour.

"We should get some rest," she murmured, breaking the spell. Luke nodded, a hint of reluctance in his eyes.

A FEW DAYS LATER, the night of the Silver Creek Christmas Rodeo arrived, and the whole town gathered at the arena. The lights glowed against the frosty air, laughter and music filling the grounds as townsfolk watched riders, ropers, and barrel racers show off their skills. Abby found herself beaming, feeling a pride she hadn't felt in a long time. She glanced over at Luke, who was watching the event with that same look of satisfaction she'd come to appreciate.

During a break, he found her by the bleachers, a playful grin on his face. "I think we make a pretty good team," he said, nodding toward the rodeo grounds. "Even if you have some, uh, unique ideas about decorating."

Abby rolled her eyes but smiled. "Guess I'll take that as a compliment."

"Good," he replied, his voice softening as he looked at her. "It was nice, having you back here. And not just for the rodeo."

Her heart skipped a beat, and for a moment, she let herself imagine staying, building a life here with him, with the ranch and her father. But as the cheering crowds reminded her of the excitement waiting in the city, a familiar hesitation settled over her.

5

Conflicts Arise

Abby stood frozen in the driveway, caught between the two men who had each, in their own way, shaped parts of her life. Alex's unexpected presence in Silver Creek was like a gust of icy wind, jolting her out of the comforting rhythm she'd just started to settle into. And Luke's piercing gaze, his jaw tight as he took in Alex's easy smile, only heightened the tension.

"Alex," she managed, stepping forward, a mix of emotions tightening her chest. "What... what are you doing here?"

Alex spread his hands, his expression smooth, almost smug. "I thought I'd surprise you," he said, glancing around at the ranch with an appreciative look that didn't quite reach his eyes. "I know you needed some time, Abby, and I wanted to give you that. But after these past few weeks... well, I realized I couldn't let things end the way they did. I still want you, Abby. I came here to see if there's still a chance for us."

Luke's expression darkened at Alex's words, his jaw clenching as he looked at Abby, an unspoken question in his eyes. She knew what he was thinking—was she going to let Alex, her polished, ambitious ex from the city, sweep her away from Silver Creek and everything they'd rekindled here? Abby took a deep breath, feeling trapped between two worlds, each pulling her in a different direction.

"I... I don't know what to say," she stammered, casting a quick glance at Luke. She could see the hurt in his eyes, and guilt twisted inside her. She hadn't told Alex that she'd moved on, that she'd found herself drawn back to her old life—and to the person who had once been her whole world.

Luke's voice broke the tense silence. "I think I'll give you two a moment," he said tersely, turning away before she could stop him. Abby felt a pang of panic as he walked back toward the barn, his shoulders rigid. She wanted to reach out, to tell him that this wasn't what it looked like, but her words caught in her throat. When she turned back to Alex, he was watching her, his expression softening.

"Abby, I know it's a lot to take in," he said gently, taking her hand in his. "But I couldn't stop thinking about you. And I don't want to lose you."

She pulled her hand away, her heart racing. "Alex... I don't know if coming here was a good idea."

He frowned, his confident demeanor faltering. "But... Abby, we've built a life together in New York. You've got your career, we had our plans... I thought maybe you'd come back with me, and we could work things out."

The words she'd once dreamed of hearing now left her cold. When she'd first met Alex, she'd been dazzled by his charm, his ambition, his ability to make anything seem possible. But standing here on her family's ranch, the home that was slipping through her father's fingers, she realized that her priorities had shifted in ways Alex couldn't understand. New York had given her success, but Silver Creek held her roots, her memories, and a different kind of future that was just beginning to take shape.

"I'm not the same person I was when I left here, Alex," she said quietly, searching his face for any sign of understanding. "This place... it's reminded me of who I am. Of who I used to be before the city."

He shook his head, disappointment shadowing his gaze. "But, Abby, this is just... a ranch. Your life is in New York now. You've worked so hard for your career; you have a future there that you'd be throwing away if you stayed here."

"Just a ranch?" The words hit her harder than she'd expected. This wasn't just any ranch; it was her father's life's work, her childhood, the only real home she'd ever known. And with Luke's help, she was starting to see a future here that could be just as fulfilling as anything she'd built in the city. For the first time, Abby felt certain of something—she wouldn't leave Silver Creek without a fight.

"Maybe you don't understand, Alex, but this place is more than just a piece of land," she said, her voice steady. "This is my family's home, our legacy. And right now, my father needs me. The ranch needs me. I'm not ready to walk away from that."

Alex's face hardened, his frustration evident. "Abby, don't do this. You don't belong here. You belong with me. Don't throw away everything we've worked for just because you feel nostalgic."

Abby's jaw tightened, a mix of anger and sadness welling up inside her. Alex's words felt like a slap, a sharp reminder of the difference between her old life and the new one she'd tried to build. But as much as she'd once cared for him, she realized that he couldn't see her for who she was now—someone who wanted more than just success and ambition. She wanted connection, purpose, a place where she truly felt at home.

"I'm sorry, Alex," she said finally, her voice barely a whisper. "But I need to stay. I have to help my father, and I need to see if there's a future for me here."

Alex's face fell, and for a brief moment, she saw real hurt in his eyes. But he quickly masked it, nodding curtly as he turned back to his car. "Fine, Abby. If that's your choice, I hope you're happy with it."

With that, he climbed into his car and drove away, leaving Abby standing alone in the driveway, her heart pounding. She knew that she'd made the right decision, but it didn't lessen the ache of realizing that a chapter of her life had truly ended. She took a shaky breath, the silence around her settling like a weight.

LATER THAT AFTERNOON, Abby found herself wandering the ranch, her thoughts a jumble of emotions. She was still processing the confrontation with Alex, the end of their relationship, and the weight of the choices she'd made. But as she walked, she found herself gravitating toward the barn, where she knew Luke would be finishing up his work for the day.

She found him there, brushing down one of the horses, his movements slow and steady. He didn't look up when she entered, but she could feel the tension radiating from him, his usual calm replaced by a stiffness she hadn't seen before.

"Luke," she began, hesitating by the doorway. "Can we talk?"

He kept his focus on the horse, his voice low and guarded. "Didn't realize you'd have time for that. Thought you'd be busy heading back to the city with your fiancé."

Abby winced, the bitterness in his tone stinging more than she'd expected. "He's not my fiancé, Luke. Not anymore. I ended it."

He glanced up then, surprise flashing in his eyes, though he quickly masked it with a neutral expression. "I see."

Abby took a deep breath, stepping closer to him. "I told him I'm staying here... at least for now. There's too much at stake, and I can't walk away from my father or the ranch. And... I don't want to walk away from everything we've started, Luke. This town, this life, it's part of who I am."

For a moment, he was silent, his gaze softening as he took in her words. "So, you're serious about staying?" he asked, a hint of hope in his voice.

"Yes, I am," she replied, feeling the truth of her decision settle within her. "I don't know exactly what the future looks like, but I know I want to give it a chance."

Luke's expression softened, his usual guardedness slipping away. "Abby, you've been my best friend, my first love. Watching you walk away all those years ago... it was one of the hardest things I've ever done." He paused, searching her eyes. "I don't want to lose you again, but I need to know you're here for real this time."

Her heart ached at his words, and she reached out, taking his hand in hers. "Luke, I'm here. And I'm not leaving this time."

The silence between them was filled with a warmth and understanding that words couldn't convey. For the first time in years, Abby felt at peace, standing with Luke in the barn, the ranch stretching out around them like a promise of the life they could build together.

As the weeks passed, Abby threw herself into the work of saving the ranch. She sat down with her father and Luke to assess the financial situation, combing through bills and bank statements as they crafted a plan to keep the ranch afloat. She reached out to old friends in the area, gathering support from the local community, and even organized a fundraiser at the town's Christmas market.

Though the workload was heavy, she found comfort in the small moments with Luke—working side by side in the fields, sharing quiet meals at the end of long days, and laughing together over the absurdities of ranch life. Their old connection grew stronger, rekindling the flame that had once been, only now deepened by the experiences they'd had apart.

One evening, as they sat by the fire in the farmhouse, Abby glanced at Luke, a warmth filling her chest. "I know this isn't the life I originally planned," she said softly, "but it feels like the right one. I think I needed to come back to Silver Creek to figure that out."

Luke smiled, taking her hand in his. "Silver Creek always had a way of showing people what really mattered. I'm just glad it brought you back to me."

They sat in comfortable silence, the crackling fire casting a warm glow over the room. Outside, snow began to fall, covering the ranch in a blanket of white, and Abby felt a peace she hadn't known she'd been searching for. In Luke's presence, with the ranch around her, she knew that she'd finally found her way home.

6

Tensions Mount

The quiet of winter had settled over Silver Creek, and the Harper ranch lay blanketed in snow, the landscape peaceful yet deceptively still. Beneath that calm, however, tensions simmered. Abby sensed it in the way Luke was quieter than usual, his gaze distant and guarded, as if he were holding back something he didn't dare say aloud.

In truth, Luke was struggling with his own fears, each one gnawing at him with growing intensity. Though Abby had stayed, his unease hadn't gone away. Seeing her here at the ranch, so naturally fitting back into the life she'd left behind, had rekindled his hope, but it also made him vulnerable. And after Alex's sudden appearance, Luke's doubts were hard to ignore. What if she left again? Worse, what if she returned to New York with her ex, leaving him and the ranch behind—again?

One cold morning, as they prepared to mend a stretch of fence along the southern pasture, Luke's frustration finally spilled over. They'd been working side by side in relative silence, the weight of their unspoken worries thick between them.

"Seems like Alex hasn't stopped trying to get you back to New York," Luke said abruptly, his tone sharper than he intended.

Abby paused, caught off guard by the comment. She glanced over, seeing the tension in his clenched jaw, the way he focused intently on the task before him. "He came here because he cares about me," she replied, though she felt a pang of guilt even as she said it. "But that doesn't mean I'm going back with him."

Luke kept his gaze on the fence post, his hands steady as he hammered in a nail. "Doesn't it?" he muttered, bitterness lacing his words. "Sometimes I wonder if you're just looking for an excuse to leave again."

Abby felt her chest tighten, hurt flaring within her. "Luke, that's not fair. You know I'm here because I want to help my dad—and I want to help you save this place."

He let out a sharp breath, dropping the hammer and turning to face her, his eyes dark with frustration. "Abby, this ranch isn't just some project you can step into whenever it suits you. It's our life out here. It's my life. And I can't keep going through this—thinking you're here for good, only to watch you walk away the moment something pulls you back to New York."

His words stung, cutting deeper than she'd expected. She opened her mouth to respond, but the truth lodged in her throat, tangled with her own insecurities. She was still torn, caught between the life she'd built in the city and the roots she felt reconnecting her to Silver Creek. And then there was Alex, constantly calling, reminding her of the career she'd put on hold, the ambitions she'd fought so hard to achieve. She felt like she was being pulled in two directions, and for the first time, she wasn't sure which path was truly hers.

"I don't know what I want yet," she admitted quietly, the

vulnerability in her words surprising even her. "Being here, with you, it feels right... but that doesn't make it easy. And Alex—he's just trying to figure things out too. Maybe I owe him that chance."

Luke's expression hardened. "So, what? You're going to spend your time here with one foot in Silver Creek and the other in New York, hedging your bets until one of us pulls you in the direction you want?"

"Luke, that's not fair—"

"Isn't it?" His voice was sharper now, the frustration spilling over in full. "I've seen you go before, Abby. You walked away from everything here, from us. And I'm supposed to believe you won't do it again? I'm not sure I can put myself through that. Not again."

Abby felt her throat tighten, but before she could respond, he turned and strode off toward the barn, leaving her standing in the cold silence, her heart racing with frustration and guilt.

OVER THE NEXT FEW DAYS, Abby threw herself into the work around the ranch, hoping to drown out the tumult of emotions that Luke's words had stirred. But as she sorted through bills and read bank statements, the reality of the ranch's financial struggles settled heavily over her. The more she saw, the clearer it became: the Harper ranch was barely staying afloat. Her father's stubborn pride had hidden just how close they were to losing it all.

The bills were endless, and as she tallied up the debts, her heart sank. Even with Luke's help, her father had fallen behind on payments, borrowing against the land just to keep things going. She could see now why Luke was frustrated; she was, too, feeling as if the weight of the entire ranch was pressing down on her shoulders. The ranch wasn't just a family legacy—it was her father's life's work. If they lost it, she wasn't sure he would recover from the heartbreak.

One afternoon, as she sorted through another stack of unpaid bills, her phone buzzed. She glanced at the screen and saw Alex's name flash across it. She hesitated, feeling a mix of dread and guilt, but eventually, she answered.

"Alex," she greeted him, her voice flat.

"Abby, I've been trying to reach you," he said, his voice exasperated but tinged with relief. "I just wanted to see how you're doing... and to talk, if you have a moment."

"Things have been... busy," she replied, glancing at the mess of papers spread out before her. "There's a lot going on here, Alex. More than I realized."

Alex was silent for a moment, and then he sighed. "Abby, you know I respect that you want to help your dad, but this is all temporary. You have a life waiting for you back in New York—a life we built together. I get that this place holds memories, but memories aren't a future. You can't stay there forever."

His words were like a splash of cold water, jolting her back to the reality she'd tried to ignore. She could feel the pull of the city, the allure of the career she'd worked so hard to build. But as she looked out the window at the snow-covered pastures, she felt an undeniable ache in her chest. Could she really leave the ranch behind, knowing how much her father had sacrificed to keep it alive?

"Alex, it's not that simple," she said finally. "I can't just walk away from this place... from my dad. It's our home. And I... I don't know if I'm ready to leave it all behind."

There was a pause on the other end of the line, and when Alex spoke again, his voice was softer, almost pleading. "Abby, I love you. I don't want to lose you to this... to a life that isn't yours anymore. Come back with me. We can find a way to make this work, I promise."

Abby's heart twisted, her mind torn between the life she'd once dreamed of and the reality in front of her. She cared for Alex; he'd been a part of her life for years, her partner in so many ways.

But her love for him felt thin compared to the depth of what she felt here, in Silver Creek, with her family—and with Luke.

"I... I need more time," she said finally, her voice barely above a whisper. She could feel the hurt in his silence, the strain in the connection that had once been so strong. But this decision wasn't something she could make lightly, not with everything she stood to lose.

"Fine," he said, his tone cold and resigned. "But I can't wait forever, Abby. Eventually, you're going to have to choose."

When the call ended, Abby sat back in her chair, the weight of the decision pressing down on her. She looked out at the ranch, the place that held her childhood, her family, and the chance for a future she hadn't been ready to admit she wanted. But the prospect of staying came with its own burdens, its own fears—and the lingering doubt that she'd let down everyone she cared about.

That evening, she found herself back in the barn, checking on the horses in the fading light. She heard footsteps behind her, and when she turned, Luke was standing in the doorway, his expression unreadable.

"I saw Alex's car in town," he said, his voice carefully neutral. "Didn't realize he was still hanging around."

Abby sighed, running a hand through her hair. "He wanted to talk. To convince me to come back to New York with him."

Luke's face darkened, and he looked away, his jaw clenched. "So, what did you tell him?"

"I told him I needed more time," she replied, searching his face. "But Luke, I... I don't want to keep hurting you. I don't want to keep dragging this out if... if it's not going anywhere."

Luke took a deep breath, his gaze intense as he finally looked at her. "Abby, I can't keep waiting, not if you're always going to be one step away from leaving. I've seen you leave before. I know what it's like to watch you walk away, to wonder if you'll ever come back." His voice softened, the vulnerability in his words cutting through her defenses. "I want you here, Abby. I want a future with you. But I need to know that you're in this for real."

Abby felt her heart ache at the raw honesty in his eyes. She wanted to give him the reassurance he needed, to tell him that she was

7

The Christmas Eve Rodeo

The chill of Christmas Eve had settled over Silver Creek, and the entire town bustled with anticipation. Strings of twinkling lights illuminated the rodeo grounds, casting a warm glow over the crisp snow blanketing the area. Abby hurried through the preparations, coordinating with volunteers as they set up tables, checked arena gates, and double-checked lighting and sound equipment. The annual Christmas Eve Rodeo was one of Silver Creek's biggest events, and despite the strain of the past few weeks, she felt a surge of pride and purpose as she watched everything fall into place.

She found herself remembering her mother, who had always made a point of making Christmas magical. The rodeo had been her mother's favorite tradition, a chance to bring the town together in celebration and give everyone a sense of belonging. Abby knew that, for her father's sake as well as her own, she had to make this rodeo unforgettable.

But the ache in her chest lingered, a reminder that this year's rodeo came with more complications than any before. Luke's words still haunted her, his fears about her leaving echoing in her mind. She hadn't realized how deeply she'd hurt him by leaving Silver Creek all those years ago. And now, with Alex pressing her to return to New York and Luke waiting for her to make a choice, she felt more torn than ever.

As she helped string a garland around the main gate, she noticed Luke checking the equipment on the far side of the arena. She hadn't spoken to him since their tense conversation, and now, as he glanced over, their eyes met. His gaze was unreadable, guarded, and yet there was a vulnerability there that struck her deeply. For a moment, she wanted nothing more than to close the distance between them, to tell him that she was ready to stay, ready to give them a real chance. But the words stayed lodged in her throat, fear and indecision holding her back.

THE HOURS FLEW by as the town gathered at the arena, bundled in scarves and coats, their faces bright with holiday excitement. Despite the cold, laughter and music filled the air, and children raced around, chasing each other with boundless energy. Abby could feel the warmth of community all around her, reminding her of everything she loved about this place.

But as she moved through the crowd, checking in with volunteers and helping with last-minute details, she noticed Luke following her path. She could sense the tension simmering between them, and finally, unable to take the silence any longer, she slipped away from the crowd and waited for him by the bleachers.

After a moment, Luke joined her, his expression a mixture of worry and frustration. For a moment, they stood in silence, the sounds of the rodeo muffled in the background. Then he spoke, his voice low and almost vulnerable.

"Abby, I need to know... Are you really staying here? Or are you going to leave as soon as things get complicated?" He paused, his gaze steady, almost pleading. "I can't keep doing this—wondering if you'll leave when something else calls you away."

Abby's heart ached at the honesty in his words, and she took a shaky breath, feeling the weight of everything she hadn't said pressing down on her. "Luke, I'm not sure what I want," she admitted, her voice barely above a whisper. "Coming back here, it reminded me of who I was before... of who I could be again. And being with you, working on the ranch, it feels so real, like I finally belong somewhere. But my life in New York... it's hard to just let that go."

Luke looked away, pain flickering in his eyes. "Abby, you can't have both. If you're going to stay, you need to stay with your whole heart. But if you're planning on leaving—" He broke off, his voice tight. "I need to know now. Because I can't keep hoping, only to watch you leave me again."

She swallowed, her own eyes filling with tears. "I don't want to hurt you, Luke. But it's not just that simple. I'm torn between what I've built and what I've come back to. And with the ranch, my dad, everything... I'm afraid of making the wrong choice. But I don't want to lose you."

His expression softened for a moment, but the pain remained, raw and deep. "Then stay, Abby. Stay here with me. We can make a life together here. This ranch—it's more than just land; it's everything I want to build a future around. But I need to know that you want this too."

Abby's heart pounded as she felt the pull of his words. She wanted to say yes, to reassure him, but the uncertainty lingered. Before she could respond, a sudden gust of icy wind swept through the arena, sending a shiver down her spine. She glanced up, noticing the darkening sky and the first few flakes of snow beginning to fall.

WITHIN MINUTES, the light snowfall turned into a full-blown snowstorm, the wind whipping through the arena as the temperature plummeted. People were huddling closer together, pulling scarves and hats tightly around themselves as the snow piled up. Abby scanned the crowd, noting the growing concern on people's faces. If the storm continued, the rodeo would be in serious jeopardy.

Luke was already on it, calling out instructions to volunteers, who scrambled to adjust the lighting and sound equipment, some running to secure the arena gates while others began helping guests find shelter under the bleachers. Abby joined him, feeling the urgency in his voice as they worked side by side, moving quickly to adapt to the situation.

As the storm intensified, Abby and Luke gathered the team, organizing the remaining volunteers to help the guests and ensure everyone's safety. The bleachers were packed as families huddled together, grateful for the temporary shelter, but Abby knew that without a quick solution, the night's rodeo was at risk of being canceled entirely.

"Everyone, listen up!" Luke's voice cut through the wind as he addressed the volunteers. "We're going to need to move everyone into the barn for shelter until the worst of the storm passes. Let's get the kids in first, and if anyone needs help, let us know. We'll figure out a way to keep this rodeo going."

Abby watched as the town rallied together, her heart swelling with pride. Parents helped their children to safety, while neighbors offered scarves and coats to those who needed extra warmth. She and Luke led the way, guiding people through the snow toward the barn, which they'd quickly transformed into a makeshift shelter. Bales of hay were laid out as seats, while a few volunteers strung extra lights to create a warm and inviting atmosphere.

Once everyone was settled, Abby helped organize a small performance area, setting up barrels and props from the rodeo for a scaled-down version of the event. The storm raged on outside, but inside the barn, the spirit of Silver Creek was alive and thriving. Children laughed as they clambered onto the hay bales, and neighbors shared stories and snacks, the warmth of community dispelling the cold.

Luke joined Abby by the entrance, wiping snow from his hat and flashing her a rare, genuine smile. "Didn't think we'd be hosting the Christmas Eve Rodeo in a barn, but I'd say it's turning out pretty well."

Abby laughed, the tension between them melting in the warmth of the moment. "Not exactly what we planned, but this might be even better."

For the next few hours, Abby and Luke took turns emceeing the rodeo, creating impromptu games and challenges for the kids, and even organizing a mock barrel race in the limited space of the barn. The crowd cheered, laughter filling the air as Silver Creek came together to celebrate, undeterred by the storm raging outside. Abby's heart felt lighter than it had in weeks, surrounded by the people she cared about in the place she'd always called home.

As the night wore on and the snowstorm finally eased, Luke found her again, his gaze soft as he looked at her. "You pulled this off, Abby. Your mom would be proud."

She felt a wave of emotion at his words, and she realized then how much she wanted to stay—not just for her father, not just for the ranch, but for the life she could build with Luke. She stepped closer, the warmth of his presence anchoring her.

"Luke," she began, her voice quiet but steady, "I'm ready to stay. I want to stay. This place, these people... and you. I'm not going anywhere."

His eyes softened, and he pulled her close, his arms wrapping around her as the weight of the past few weeks seemed to melt away. For the first time, Abby felt like she'd finally found where she belonged. Silver Creek, with its snowy pastures, the warmth of community, and the quiet strength of the man beside her—it was her home.

As they stood together in the glow of the barn lights, the echoes of laughter and cheers all around, Abby knew that this Christmas Eve would be the first of many to come. And as the snow continued to fall softly outside, she felt certain of one thing: she was finally, truly home.

8

A Cowboy's Confession

The storm had finally eased, and as the last snowflakes drifted gently from the sky, Silver Creek was transformed into a scene from a Christmas postcard. The town had rallied together in a way that Abby had only ever seen in Silver Creek. The barn, once just a shelter from the storm, had become a warm gathering place, buzzing with laughter and celebration as families and friends huddled together on hay bales, sipping hot cocoa and swapping stories.

Yet, with the snow easing, people were drawn outside, pulled by the sight of the snow-covered rodeo arena glittering under the moonlight. The heavy snowfall had left a thick, pristine layer across the grounds, and as Abby joined Luke by the entrance, she marveled at the magic of the moment. Twinkling lights lined the fences, and lanterns dotted the perimeter, casting a soft glow that reflected off the snow and wrapped the entire scene in a golden, ethereal light.

"It's perfect," Abby whispered, a sense of awe filling her.

Luke smiled beside her, his eyes as warm as the glow around them. "Couldn't have planned it better ourselves."

The townsfolk began to filter back out to the arena, their excitement and relief evident. For a moment, Abby caught sight of her father, Bill, leaning on his cane and looking out over the scene with a contented smile. She knew how much this night meant to him, how it honored her mother's memory, and a wave of pride filled her heart. The Christmas Eve Rodeo was back on, and thanks to everyone's efforts, it would be one to remember.

WITH THE SOUND of fiddles and laughter in the background, the rodeo kicked off, bringing smiles to faces young and old. Cowboys and cowgirls paraded their horses around the arena, each of them waving to the crowd as their breath steamed in the cold night air. The snow only added to the magic, each fall of hooves kicking up sparkling flakes.

Abby joined the crowd, taking part in the excitement and laughter as she cheered on local riders. She saw families gathered together, friends reunited, and neighbors helping one another, and a deep sense of belonging washed over her. It was a feeling she'd never found in the city, and it tugged at her heart with a quiet but undeniable certainty.

Midway through the event, there was a pause in the festivities as a few of the organizers gathered to announce the funds raised from the night. The community had come together in an outpouring of generosity, and the amount collected was beyond anything Abby had expected. Enough, she realized, to make a significant dent in her father's financial troubles, and a wave of relief and gratitude overwhelmed her.

The announcer's voice echoed across the arena, ringing with pride. "Tonight, thanks to everyone here, we've raised enough money to help support the Harper ranch and preserve a piece of Silver Creek's history for generations to come!"

Applause erupted, and Abby felt herself swept into the crowd as people clapped her on the back, congratulating her and sharing in the joy. Her eyes met her father's across the crowd, and she saw the shimmer of tears in his eyes, a pride that filled her heart with warmth.

But as the cheering quieted, Abby felt a presence beside her. She turned to see Luke, his expression soft, the glow from the lights reflecting in his eyes.

"Come with me," he murmured, holding out his hand.

Curious, Abby slipped her hand into his, letting him lead her through the snow and past the cheering crowd, out to the far end of the arena where they stood beneath a string of lights. The world around them was still and quiet, the sound of laughter and music fading into the background.

For a moment, they stood in silence, and Abby felt her heart pounding, anticipation filling her as she looked up at him. Snowflakes drifted down around them, catching in Luke's hair and on his coat, and the whole world seemed to hold its breath.

"Abby," he began, his voice low, full of something that made her pulse quicken. "I've wanted to tell you this for a long time. When you left Silver Creek, it was like a part of me went with you. I tried to move on, to accept that you had bigger dreams, that you were meant for something outside this town. But I couldn't forget you, Abby. I never did."

She felt her breath catch as he continued, his gaze steady, filled with a warmth and vulnerability that cut through every doubt she'd held.

"Seeing you here again, working on this ranch, making tonight happen... it reminded me of everything I've ever wanted. Abby, I love you. I've loved you since we were kids, and I've been waiting for you ever since. And I'm here for you, always—whether you stay or go. I just had to tell you, no matter what."

For a moment, Abby was speechless, her heart full to bursting. She'd always known that Luke cared for her, but hearing him say it, here under the falling snow and surrounded by the people she loved, made everything fall into place. She realized, in that moment, that she didn't need New York or the life she'd built there to feel whole. She'd been searching for a sense of belonging, a place where she was truly loved, and it was right here in Silver Creek.

"Luke," she whispered, her voice breaking, "I love you, too. I think I always have. And I know now that... this is where I'm meant to be. Here, with you, with my family, with this town."

She felt his arms wrap around her, pulling her close as the world seemed to fade away, leaving only the two of them standing together beneath the lights, snow drifting down around them like a blessing. Their kiss was gentle, full of all the love and longing they'd held back for so long, and Abby felt a peace she hadn't known she'd been searching for settle deep in her heart.

As they stood there together, wrapped in each other's arms, Abby knew that she'd finally come home.

9

A Cowboy's Confession

The storm had finally passed, leaving Silver Creek transformed under a blanket of pristine snow. The twinkling lights that lined the rodeo arena shone brighter against the snow-covered backdrop, casting a warm glow over the crowd gathered for the annual Christmas Eve Rodeo. The town had pulled together, and despite the challenges, the event was alive with holiday cheer and community spirit.

Abby moved through the crowd, helping set up last-minute details with a sense of purpose and pride. This wasn't just any Christmas Eve Rodeo—this one was special, bringing Silver Creek together after so many struggles. Abby's heart felt fuller than ever, though she couldn't shake the tension that had built between her and Luke. She hadn't spoken to him since their emotional confrontation, and the hurt in his eyes haunted her. He'd laid his feelings bare, and she was left facing the weight of his confession and her own conflicting desires.

As she adjusted the lights on a nearby post, Abby saw Luke across the arena, talking to her father. For a moment, he looked over, and their eyes met. His gaze held a quiet intensity, and Abby felt her heart quicken. But before she could move, her father gave her a reassuring nod, silently encouraging her forward. She took a deep breath and headed over to them, a mixture of anticipation and apprehension coursing through her.

"Luke," she said softly as she reached him, her breath visible in the cold night air. Her father gave them both a knowing smile and slipped away, leaving them alone in the snowy glow of the arena.

They stood in silence, the world around them blurring into the background. Finally, Luke spoke, his voice low and steady. "Abby, I've been holding onto this for too long. I thought I could wait forever, that I'd always be ready for you, whenever you decided to come back. But seeing you here again, I can't hold it back any longer."

She felt her pulse race as he took a step closer, his gaze fixed on hers with an intensity that left her breathless. "I love you, Abby. I've always loved you. And I can't pretend anymore that I don't want you here. Not just for tonight, not just for the holidays. For good."

Abby felt a flood of emotions rising within her, her heart aching as she looked up at him. Everything she'd felt—the pull of the city, the memories of Silver Creek, the life she'd built and the one she'd left behind—collided in her mind, leaving her unsteady.

"Luke, I..." Her voice faltered, caught between the truth of her feelings and the weight of her fears. "I don't know if I'm ready to leave New York behind. There's so much I still need to figure out, and I—"

Her words were cut off as the arena lights flickered, and a murmur swept through the crowd. The speakers crackled as the announcer's voice came over the PA system, bringing everyone's attention back to the rodeo.

But before she could turn, Luke reached for her hand, his grip firm but gentle. "Abby, please... don't do this halfway. Don't leave me waiting."

Abby opened her mouth to answer, but her thoughts scattered as the crowd's cheers suddenly turned into startled gasps. People began pointing toward the distant hills, where an eerie glow had appeared against the snowy backdrop.

"What's going on?" she whispered, but Luke's expression had turned grim.

Without answering, he tightened his hold on her hand and led her through the crowd, weaving past people until they reached the edge of the arena. The glow from the hills had intensified, and Abby's heart sank as she recognized the unmistakable sight of flames dancing against the dark sky.

"Oh, no," she breathed, realization dawning on her. "The ranch..."

Luke's jaw clenched as he glanced back toward the crowd. "It looks like something's happened up there. I need to go check on it, make sure your father's place is safe."

"I'm coming with you," Abby said, determination filling her voice.

But Luke hesitated, his hand lingering on hers. "Abby, you don't have to do this. If it's dangerous—"

She shook her head, her voice steady. "This is my home, too. I'm not letting you go alone."

He searched her face, and for a brief moment, Abby thought she saw something soften in his eyes. Then, with a nod, he pulled her close, pressing a quick, desperate kiss to her forehead before leading her toward the truck parked by the fence.

As they sped up the snow-dusted road, the glow on the horizon grew brighter, filling Abby with a cold dread that settled deep in her bones. She looked over at Luke, his face set with grim determination, and realized that this wasn't just a fire threatening the land—this was a test of everything they'd built, everything they stood to lose.

As they rounded the bend and saw the flames licking dangerously close to the Harper ranch, Abby knew one thing for certain: tonight, they'd have to fight for the life they wanted together. And as they faced the blaze illuminating the snowy landscape, her heart pounded with the fear that it might already be too late.

10

A Christmas Decision

The night's events weighed heavily on Abby as she leaned against the barn wall, watching the last remnants of smoke rise against the snow-blanketed hills. Thanks to the town's swift response, the fire had been contained before it could reach the heart of the ranch, but the scare had shaken her to the core. She'd come so close to losing everything—her father's land, the memories of her mother, and the chance for a life she was only now realizing she wanted.

As dawn broke over Silver Creek, casting a soft pink glow over the ranch, Abby's father emerged from the barn, leaning on his cane with a warm but weary smile.

"You alright, sweetheart?" he asked, his voice gentle.

Abby managed a smile, though her heart was still racing. "I think so, Dad. It just... it felt like we almost lost it all last night."

Bill nodded, looking out at the ranch, the land he'd spent his life caring for. "This place means a lot to me, Abby. But more than anything, I've always wanted you to find a life that brings you joy." He paused, studying her with a knowing look. "I thought that life might be in the city, but... maybe it's here. With Luke. I see it every time I look at you two together."

She glanced down, her heart stirring at the mention of Luke. Bill's words hit closer to home than he knew, uncovering a truth she'd tried to ignore for too long. "I always thought I needed more, that I had to leave to find myself. But being here, seeing everything and everyone come together last night..." She looked up at her father, her voice barely above a whisper. "This is where I belong. I know that now."

Bill reached out, squeezing her hand, his eyes shining with pride and understanding. "Then don't let anything take you away from it, Abby. You deserve to be happy, and you deserve a love that'll stay with you."

A rush of emotion overwhelmed her, and she hugged him tightly, feeling the strength of her father's presence and the steady comfort of home. When she pulled back, she felt a new certainty filling her heart. She knew what she had to do.

THE SUN WAS SETTING as Abby made her way back to the rodeo grounds, now dusted in fresh snow. The arena was quieter, filled only with the sounds of townsfolk sharing stories, children laughing, and people hugging one another after a night they'd remember for years. The warm glow of Christmas lights lined the fences, casting a golden hue over the snowy landscape.

As she reached the edge of the arena, her eyes landed on Luke, standing beneath a string of lights, his expression distant as he gazed across the arena. Abby's heart raced, her steps light as she made her way over to him.

"Luke," she called softly, and he turned, surprise flickering in his eyes as she approached.

"Abby," he said, his voice steady, but his eyes betrayed a glimmer of hope. "You're back."

She nodded, her heart pounding with the words she'd been waiting to say. "I had to see you, Luke. There's something I need to tell you." She took a deep breath, the words tumbling out. "I'm staying. Here in Silver Creek, with you, with my dad, with the life we could build together. I don't want to run anymore. This is my home. And you... you're who I want by my side."

For a moment, Luke's expression softened, and then he took her hands in his, his gaze searching hers. "You mean that? You're really staying?"

She nodded, her heart full as she held his gaze. "Yes. I'm done chasing something that was never right for me. I'm staying here, with you, because this is where I belong."

A slow, grateful smile spread across Luke's face, his eyes shining with warmth as he gently pulled her close. "You don't know how long I've waited to hear you say that."

And then, under the glow of Christmas lights, surrounded by the love and laughter of their community, Luke leaned down, capturing her lips in a tender, heartfelt kiss that felt like a promise of everything to come. Abby felt herself melt into the moment, her worries, her doubts, all slipping away, leaving only the certainty of his love and the warmth of the life they could share together.

As they broke apart, cheers erupted from nearby, and Abby turned to see the townsfolk clapping and smiling, some wiping away tears as they watched. Her cheeks flushed, but she felt nothing but joy and contentment as the crowd gathered around them, sharing in the celebration of their new beginning.

"Looks like the town approves," Luke said with a grin, pulling her close as they turned to watch the festivities around them.

A band began playing Christmas carols, filling the air with music as couples swayed to the rhythm, children tossed snowballs, and friends laughed together. Abby glanced up as snow began to fall softly, blanketing the scene in a light, sparkling dust.

She looked up at Luke, her heart swelling as she held his gaze. "Thank you, for waiting for me. For believing in us."

He shook his head, his eyes full of warmth. "You were worth every moment, Abby. I'd wait a lifetime if it meant I got to share it with you."

As the snow fell around them and the town celebrated the success of the rodeo and the reunion of two people who'd finally found their way back to each other, Abby felt, for the first time in her life, truly at home. And with Luke by her side, she knew that their future, however uncertain, was one she was ready to embrace.

In that perfect Western Christmas scene, they stood together, surrounded by the laughter and warmth of a town that had always known where Abby's heart belonged—even when she hadn't.

11

Epilogue – A Year Later

Snow blanketed the fields, transforming the Harper ranch into a winter wonderland that seemed to glow under the pale December sun. Abby stood on the front porch, watching the soft flakes drift from the sky, her heart filled with a quiet joy that had come to feel as familiar as the ranch itself. It was Christmas Eve once again, and this year, Silver Creek's holiday celebration was set to be held at the Harper ranch, marking a new tradition for the town and for her growing family.

INSIDE, the house buzzed with activity and laughter. Friends, neighbors, and family filled the cozy space, gathered around the fireplace or helping themselves to steaming mugs of cider and slices of her father's favorite pecan pie. Bill was leaning back in his armchair, chuckling at a story from one of the ranch hands, his face more relaxed and content than Abby had seen in years. It filled her with pride knowing she had helped secure this future for him—and for the generations yet to come.

As the door creaked open, Abby turned to see Luke walking in, his face bright with the cold, his eyes finding hers with a look that made her heart skip a beat even now. He walked over, a familiar warmth in his gaze as he held up a sprig of mistletoe.

"Mistletoe, Miss Harper?" he asked, his voice low and teasing.

She laughed, letting him pull her into a kiss, her heart still fluttering with the thrill of their love. And as she pulled back, her eyes fell to the beautiful engagement ring on her hand, a simple, elegant piece with a small emerald at its center—Luke's nod to the color of her eyes.

THEIR ENGAGEMENT HAD BEEN the talk of the town, and in the months since, they'd taken to running both his ranch and the Harper ranch together. With Abby's business skills and Luke's practical know-how, they'd modernized operations, bringing in new equipment, digital records, and even some strategic marketing to attract new clients. Their efforts had transformed both properties into sustainable businesses, ensuring that the land and legacy would endure.

"Is everything ready outside?" Abby asked, glancing out the window toward the barn, where tables had been set up for the evening's celebration.

Luke nodded, a warm smile tugging at his lips. "Everything's perfect. Just waiting for you, soon-to-be Mrs. Grayson."

Her heart leapt at the sound of her new name, the future they were about to build together. The past year had been filled with hard work, learning, and growth, but with each day, she'd felt herself grow deeper roots here, in the place she'd once left behind.

New York felt like a lifetime ago, a dream that had faded, replaced by something truer and more lasting.

THEY JOINED the crowd in the barn, which was aglow with lanterns, twinkling lights, and the warmth of holiday spirit. Children raced around, playing hide-and-seek in the hay bales, while families and friends gathered, sharing stories and laughter, everyone basking in the sense of togetherness that had come to define Silver Creek.

As the night wore on, Abby took a quiet moment, leaning against the barn wall and looking out over the gathering, her heart brimming with gratitude. She had everything she'd once thought she'd find in the city: fulfillment, purpose, and a love that made her feel fully seen, fully cherished.

Her father approached her, his eyes twinkling with pride. "You did good, kid," he said, wrapping an arm around her shoulder.

Abby leaned her head against him, feeling the comfort of his presence. "Thanks, Dad. I guess I needed to find my way back here to figure it all out."

Bill chuckled, his gaze sweeping over the barn, filled with the people who had become their extended family. "This ranch was always part of you, Abby. Just had to realize it in your own time."

She smiled, knowing he was right. She had found herself here in Silver Creek, not by chasing dreams, but by letting go of them and discovering the happiness in front of her.

ACROSS THE ROOM, she caught Luke's eye, and he made his way over to her, his smile as warm and true as it had been that night under the Christmas lights. He took her hand, lacing their fingers together.

"To the future, Abby," he murmured, his eyes bright with love.

"To our future," she replied, leaning into his embrace as the crowd around them celebrated, laughter and music filling the air, snow falling softly outside. And as she stood there, with her father, her friends, her love, and her home around her, Abby knew she was exactly where she was meant to be.

Her journey had come full circle, and now, surrounded by everything she'd once tried to leave behind, she was finally, truly home.

Also by James Holloway

Short Stories Of Christmas Nostalgic Christmas Stories From The 1950s to 1980s

DREAMLAND Christmas Love Story in 1950s Hollywood

The Silent Season: A 1950s Christmas Tale of Love, Loss, and Hope